Leaping Lola

For my parents, who endured dynamic leaping and twirling throughout the house during my many years of ballet dancing.
~ T H

For Angela and Rob.
~ A T

First published in the UK in 2019
This edition printed in 2020 by New Frontier Publishing Europe Ltd
Uncommon, 126 New King's Rd, Fulham SW6 4LZ
www.newfrontierpublishing.co.uk

Text copyright © 2019 Tracey Hawkins • Illustrations copyright © 2019 Anil Tortop
The moral rights of the author and illustrator have been asserted.
All characters and events in this publication, other than those clearly
in the public domain, are fictitious and any resemblance to
real persons, living or dead, is purely coincidental.
All rights reserved.

A CIP catalogue record for this book
is available from the British Library.
ISBN: 978-1-912858-52-1

Designed by Verity Clark

Printed and bound in China
1 3 5 7 9 10 8 6 4 2

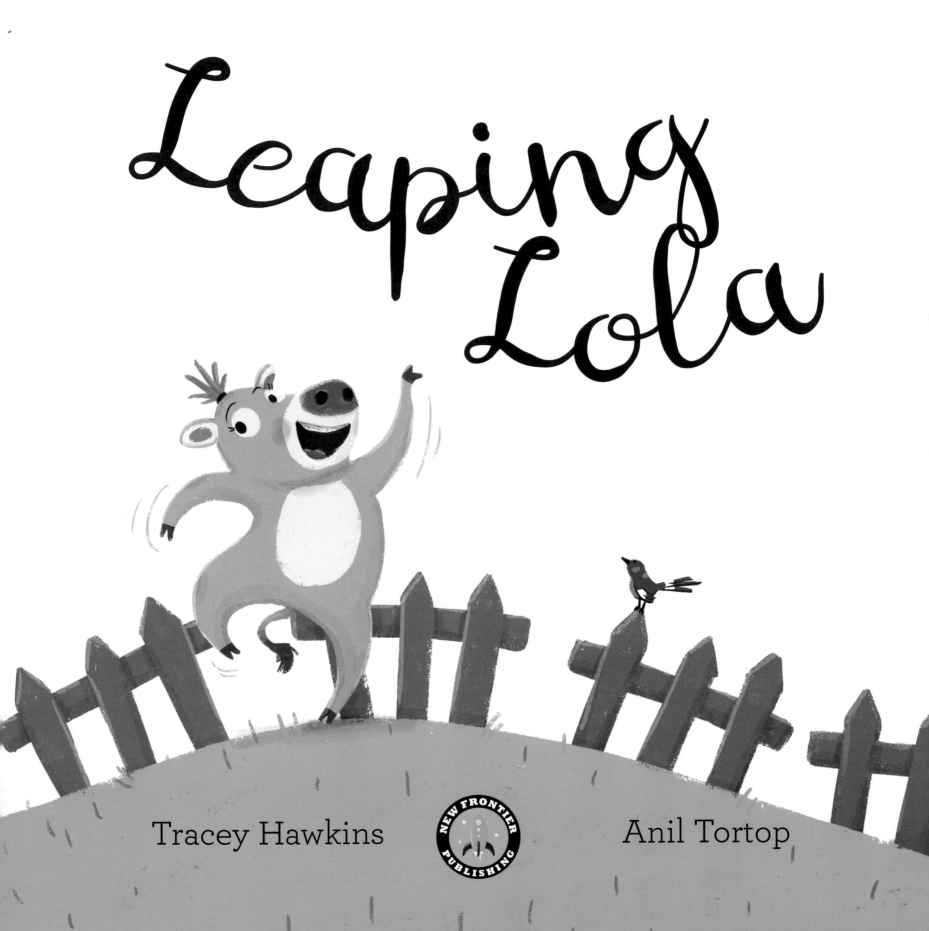

Leaping Lola

Tracey Hawkins

Anil Tortop

Down in the meadow, all boggy with mud,
Clarissa the cow was chewing her cud.

Up on the hilltop a calf caught her eye:
Flouncing and **bouncing**, she frolicked on by.

'Oh no!' cried Clarissa.
'Lola, don't **prance**.
Jerseys are milk cows –
we're not built to dance.'

'I can't help it, Mother, try as I might –
I need to **practise** for the ball tonight!'

High on back haunches,

clip-clopping her **hooves,**

Lola **flicked** up her tail

in **fabulous** moves.

A pirouette here, a **pirouette** there,

Spiralling up with the **wind** in her hair.

But down in the milk shed, chomping on hay,
Lola's plans for the ball **slithered** away.
'No **dance** for you,' said Mother with a **frown**.
'It's the **Black** and **White** Ball . . . and you are **brown**.'

Flopped in the **slop** of her friend Pearl's pigsty,
Lola told her **sad** tale and had a good **cry**.

'I have an idea,' **squealed** Pearl in delight.
'If you want to go, I'll **dress** you just right.'

At the barn door,
Lola **sashayed** on in,
Flashing the doorman
a big toothy grin.

The twang of the band made her **wriggle** and **giggle**,
Her neck gave a **nod**, her bottom a **jiggle**.

Swishing her tail to the **beat** of the bass,

Lola **rose** on her **toes** with **exquisite** grace,

Whoomping and **boomping** her bountiful hide

And crossing the floor

with a **SWOOP** and a **slide.**

Mad for the music, she **kicked up** her heels,

Wowing the crowd with **extravagant** reels.

Enthralled by the tunes, she **soared** in the air,

Swirling and **twirling** her large derrière.

Then missing her landing, **falling** and **gliding**,
She parted the herd, **slipping** and **sliding**.

Smash, bash, crash!

Lola knocked the milk tower,

Splish, splosh, splash!
came the gushing white shower.

The downpour of milk washed mud from her hide,
Swamping the guests in the flood of the tide.
The cows were in chaos, mooing in fright:

'There's an **imposter** among us tonight.'

A deep voice **boomed** from the rear of the hall,
As the prize-winning bull **stormed** from his stall.

'All cows want to dance,
no matter their breed.
Dance for us, Lola,
we'll follow your lead.'

Laughing with glee, Lola took to the floor,
Bounding with vigour as never before.

She led the line dancing, **sloshing** in mud,
With a **romp** and a **stomp** and a **thump** and a **thud**.

When dawn broke the night, cows swaggered away.
Contented, they snoozed upon mounds of soft hay.
But up on a hill, with a **twist** and a **twirl**,
Lola was **leaping** with her best friend Pearl.